Transportation & Communication Series

Airplanes

Arlene Bourgeois Molzahn

 **Enslow Publishers, Inc.**

40 Industrial Road   PO Box 38
Box 398   Aldershot
Berkeley Heights, NJ 07922   Hants GU12 6BP
USA   UK

http://www.enslow.com

To my granddaughter Elizabeth, who is such a joy, and to her Uncle Mike who is an airplane pilot.

Copyright © 2003 by Enslow Publishers, Inc.

All rights reserved.

No part of this book may be reproduced by any means without the written permission of the publisher.

Library of Congress Cataloging-in-Publication Data

Molzahn, Arlene Bourgeois.
   Airplanes / Arlene Bourgeois Molzahn.
      v. cm. — (Transportation & communication series)
   Includes bibliographical references and index.
   Contents: Two great pilots—Many kinds of airplanes—History of flight—Airplanes and airports—Many, many jobs—Newer, bigger, better, faster—Timeline.
   ISBN 0-7660-2026-6
   1. Airplanes—Juvenile literature. 2. Aeronautics—Juvenile literature. [1. Airplanes. 2. Aeronautics.] I. Title. II. Series.
TL547 .M642 2002
629.13—dc21   2002004379

Printed in the United States of America

10 9 8 7 6 5 4 3 2 1

To Our Readers: We have done our best to make sure all Internet Addresses in this book were active and appropriate when we went to press. However, the author and the publisher have no control over and assume no liability for the material available on those Internet sites or on other Web sites they may link to. Any comments or suggestions can be sent by e-mail to comments@enslow.com or to the address on the back cover.

Every effort has been made to locate all copyright holders of material used in this book. If any errors or omissions have occurred, corrections will be made in future editions of this book.

Illustration Credits: Courtesy of the American Institute of Aeronautics and Astronautics, Inc., p. 20 (bottom); Amanda Brown/*The Star Ledger*, p. 30 (top); Frank H. Conlon/*The Star Ledger*, p. 42 (bottom); Corel Corporation, pp. 10, 13, 15, 16 (top), 17 (bottom), 24, 34, 38, 40, 41; Dover Publications, p. 19, 20 (top); Aris Economopoulos/*The Star Ledger*, pp. 32, 37 (bottom); Enslow Publishers, Inc., p. 6 (bottom); Enslow Publishers, Inc. diagram using Corel Corporation image, p. 26 (top); Chris Faytok/*The Star Ledger*, p. 31 (bottom); Hemera Technologies, Inc. 1997-2000, pp. 1, 2, 5, 11, 12 (bottom), 14 (bottom), 16 (bottom), 17 (top), 25, 26 (bottom), 31 (top), 33, 35 (bottom), 39, 42 (top); Star Ledger photo by Tom Kitts, p. 12 (top); Star Ledger photo by Rich Krauss, p. 29 (top); Tony Kurdzuk/*The Star Ledger*, p. 29 (bottom); Library of Congress, pp. 4, 6 (top), 8, 9, 18, 21; Scott Lituchy/*The Star Ledger*, p. 14 (top); NASA Langley, p. 43; Kristin McCarthy, p. 36; National Archives, pp. 22, 23; *New York Herald Tribune*, p. 7; John O'Boyle/*The Star Ledger*, p. 27; *Star Ledger* photo by Richard Raska, p. 28; Patti Sapone/*The Star Ledger*, p. 37 (top); Lexey Swall/*The Star Ledger*, p. 30 (bottom); VicYepello/*The Star Ledger*, p. 35 (top).

Cover Illustration: © Corel Corporation.

Contents

1 Two Great Pilots 5

2 Many Kinds of Airplanes 11

3 History of Flight 19

4 Airplanes and Airports 25

5 Many, Many Jobs 33

6 Newer, Bigger, Better, Faster 39

Timeline 44

Words to Know 46

Learn More About Airplanes
(Books and Internet Addresses) 47

Index 48

Chapter 1

Two Great Pilots

Airplanes are amazing machines. The people who fly them are even more amazing. Charles A. Lindbergh was the first man to fly across the Atlantic Ocean. Amelia Earhart wanted to be the first woman to fly around the world. During the early days of flying, Lindbergh and Earhart were pioneers.

Charles A. Lindbergh

On May 21, 1927, over 150,000 people gathered at an airfield near Paris, France. They were waiting for the airplane *Spirit of St. Louis*. Charles A. Lindbergh was the pilot. He was flying the plane by himself across the Atlantic Ocean from New York City.

Charles A. Lindbergh (left) stands in front of his airplane.

Charles A. Lindbergh flew his *Spirit of St. Louis* across the Atlantic Ocean.

Lindbergh started his flight in New York and ended in Paris, France.

In 1919, a man from New York had made an offer to pilots. He would give $25,000 to the first pilot who could fly nonstop from New York to Paris.

By 1927, no one had won the money. Lindbergh wanted to try. He helped build his own special airplane. He wanted to keep the airplane as light he as could. He decided not to carry a radio or a parachute.

On May 20, people cheered as Lindbergh took off. He planned to fly over 3,600 miles. He had 400 gallons of gasoline, five sandwiches, and one quart of water with him. He would have to fly the plane for many hours without sleeping to reach Paris.

Lindbergh almost fell asleep a few times. He had to fly through fog and clouds of ice. But after more

Lindbergh made front page headlines in many newspapers.

than 33 ½ hours of flying, he landed safely in France.

Charles Lindbergh will be remembered as the first person to fly by himself, or solo, across the Atlantic Ocean. He was one of our first great airplane pilots.

Amelia Mary Earhart

In 1920, twenty-three year-old Amelia Earhart took her first airplane ride. It was then she knew she wanted to be a pilot. She soon began taking flying lessons. In 1922, Earhart flew her airplane to a record height of 14,000 feet. In 1928, she flew a solo flight across the United States. Five years after Lindbergh's flight to Paris in 1932, Earhart became the first woman to fly solo across the Atlantic Ocean. In 1935, she flew from Hawaii to California and then on to Washington D.C. All these flights were records for women pilots. Next, Earhart wanted to be the first woman to fly around the world.

On June 1, 1937, Earhart left on what she said would be her last long flight. She started by flying east from Miami, Florida. She planned to go around the world. She took a navigator, Fred Noonan, with her to help her along the way.

They had no trouble for the first 22,000

Amelia Earhart wanted to be the first woman to fly around the world.

miles. On July 2, they had only 7,000 miles to go. Earhart's plane, the *Electra*, took off from New Guinea heading for the United States.

On that same day, the United States Coast Guard ship *Itasca* was patrolling the Pacific Ocean. About nineteen hours after the *Electra* took off, the ship received a radio message. It was from the *Electra*. The message said, "Gas is running low."

The ship sent a message to the *Electra*. There was no answer. Soon the ship began to search for the plane. The *Electra* and the two pilots were not found. It is believed that the airplane crashed in the ocean.

Amelia Earhart will always be remembered as one of our first great women pilots.

Before Amelia Earhart took off on her famous flight, many people checked her airplane.

Here, Earhart takes off.

Chapter 2

Many Kinds of Airplanes

Today we have many different kinds of airplanes. There are passenger planes, military planes, cargo planes, and special purpose planes.

The Boeing 747 is one of the busiest passenger planes. It can carry up to 500 people. It has four jet engines and can fly without stopping for 6,000 miles. It can travel at speeds of almost 600 miles per hour (mph). It carries over 47,000 gallons of fuel. Planes that carry passengers and a small amount of cargo are called airliners.

There are many different types of airplanes. This one pictured left is a Boeing 747.

Airplanes need a lot of fuel. This man is helping refuel an airplane.

The Concorde is one of the fastest planes. It is a supersonic airliner. It is called supersonic because it can fly faster than the speed of sound. The speed of sound travels about 760 mph at sea level. The speed of sound is about 750 mph at the height an airplane flies. The Concorde can fly at almost 1,400 mph. Whenever this plane flies faster than the speed of sound, it causes a sonic boom. A sonic boom sounds like a clap of thunder to people on the ground. The Concorde can carry 128 passengers.

Many passenger planes are not as big as the Boeing 747 or as fast as the Concorde. Most airliners carry from 100 to 250 passengers, and they also carry light cargo.

Cargo planes are made to carry all kinds of goods, or cargo. These planes do not have seats for passengers. Instead, the inside of the plane is like a huge room. Air cargo can be almost anything including trucks, machinery, fresh foods, and flowers.

The Concorde can fly very fast. The speed of sound is about 750 mph at the height an airplane flies. The Concorde can fly faster than that.

Airplanes have room to carry many things. These people are loading an airliner.

Usually things that must be shipped in a hurry are shipped by air. Airplanes are the fastest and the most expensive way to ship cargo.

There are many types of military planes. A small number of military planes were used in World War I. Military planes were improved and were very important in World War II. Today the armed forces have planes that can attack enemy forces, protect our troops on the ground, and bring in supplies. They defend the country from enemies, and they help keep the peace. Jet fighter planes can fly nonstop from one country to another in just a few hours.

Some airplanes are used to fight forest fires. The inside of the plane is really a large tank that can hold many gallons of water. The water is poured on the fire as the airplane flies over the burning area. Sometimes planes carry special chemicals to put on fires to put them out.

Military airplanes became important during World War II. Shown below is a Lockheed P-38 Lightning and a WWII Jenny biplane (inset).

Airplanes can be very helpful when fighting forest fires. They can fly over the fire and drop water to help put it out.

Crop dusters are small airplanes used on large farms. These airplanes can dust or spray the crops to help fight bugs or diseases. They can also spread fertilizer on the land. Some companies use small planes to check power lines and pipelines.

Seaplanes are planes that have floats instead of wheels. The floats make it possible for the planes to land and take off on water. Seaplanes are used to carry passengers between small islands. They are used to bring people to places where there are lakes but no airports. Many scientists and adventure travelers use seaplanes to fly to places that are hard to reach.

Most airplanes need a runway to take off. The engine is used to make the plane go down the runway very fast. The air rushes over the wings and lifts the airplane off the ground. Big airplanes need much longer runways than small planes.

Planes that have floats instead of wheels can land on water.

Chapter 3

History of Flight

Leonardo da Vinci.

Long ago people watched birds flying in the sky. They wanted to fly, too. Some people tied feathers to their arms and tried to fly. But most people believed that flying was something only birds could do.

Leonardo da Vinci was a gifted inventor and painter who lived in Italy from 1452 to 1519. He drew up plans for a helicopter, an airplane, and a parachute. Many years later his drawings gave other inventors ideas on how to build them.

In the 1700s, the Montgolfier brothers in France built the first working hot-air balloon.

Many people were interested in flying. During the 1700s, they experimented with hydrogen-filled balloons (left).

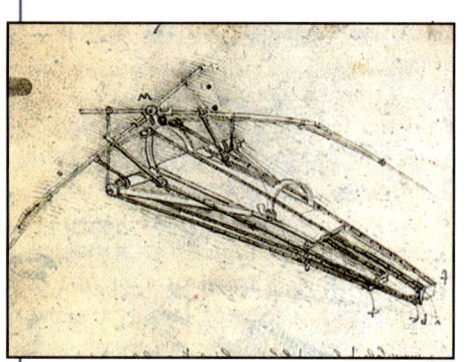

Leonardo da Vinci invented many things. This is his sketch of a helicopter.

The Montgolfier brothers built the first working hot-air balloon, shown here.

It was a large balloon made of paper and cloth. They made a fire and filled the balloon with hot air. Hot air is lighter than cold air. It rises above cold air. The hot air trapped in the balloon caused it to rise.

In October 1783, Frenchman Jean-François Pilâtre de Rozier became the first person to fly in a hot-air balloon. Later that year, he and François-Laurent d'Arlandes made the first long flight in a balloon. They stayed in the air for about twenty-five minutes and traveled more than five miles over Paris. Many more experiments were made with hot-air balloons. But balloons were hard to control in windy weather. They were also slow and hard to steer.

Many people tried different ways to make flying machines. But they did not work well.

Orville and Wilbur Wright were brothers who lived in Dayton, Ohio. They made bicycles. They also read and studied as much as they could about flying machines. *Flyer* was the name of the first airplane the Wright brothers built. On December 17, 1903, in Kitty Hawk, North Carolina, Orville Wright flew the *Flyer*. The airplane flew 120 feet at about thirty miles per hour. The flight lasted only twelve seconds but it was the first successful airplane flight in the world. Later that day, Wilbur made a flight of 852 feet and it lasted fifty-nine seconds. That was the beginning of aviation, as we know it today.

Orville and Wilbur Wright began their flying experiments by building gliders, like these below.

Airplanes were used to fly mail to distant cities. This photo, taken in the 1940s, shows a plane with snow skiis so it could land in snowy areas.

During World War II, many areas of work were open to women. This mechanic works on an airplane engine.

In 1909, Louis Blériot flew an airplane across the English Channel from France to England. This was the first sea crossing in an airplane.

Airplanes continued to be improved. However, most still had only one engine. Airplanes were used mostly to attract crowds. People enjoyed watching air shows and air races. Both men and women would do daring tricks with small airplanes. These tricks were very dangerous, and many flyers lost their lives.

In World War I, both sides used airplanes to help locate enemy troops and military bases. Later, airplanes began carrying bombs in a bag inside the plane. The bombs were dropped over the side of the plane on the enemy. Then, planes called bombers were built. They carried the bombs under the body and wings of the airplane. Now men in the planes had more control over where the bombs could be dropped.

Here, an airplane is about to land on an aircraft carrier after an air strike during World War II.

After the war, the first large passenger planes were built. They had chairs for people to sit on. But the engines were so loud that passengers could not talk to each other. The planes had no heat so passengers were always cold. Many, many things were done to make airplanes better. Today, we have large comfortable jet planes that fly to all parts of the world.

Chapter 4

Airplanes and Airports

The *Flyer* of the Wright Brothers was made of wood, wire, and cloth. Airplanes are very different today. Bigger airplanes can have two or four jet engines. They have two long sleek wings. The outside edges of the wings can move up and down. These movable parts are called ailerons. Ailerons roll the plane in the direction the pilot wants to go. A part of the tail sticks up in the back of the plane and can move left and right. This part is called the rudder. The rudder turns the plane in the direction the pilot wants it to go. Airplanes have landing gear made of either wheels or floats. The landing

This plane (left) takes off as the bus heads to the airport.

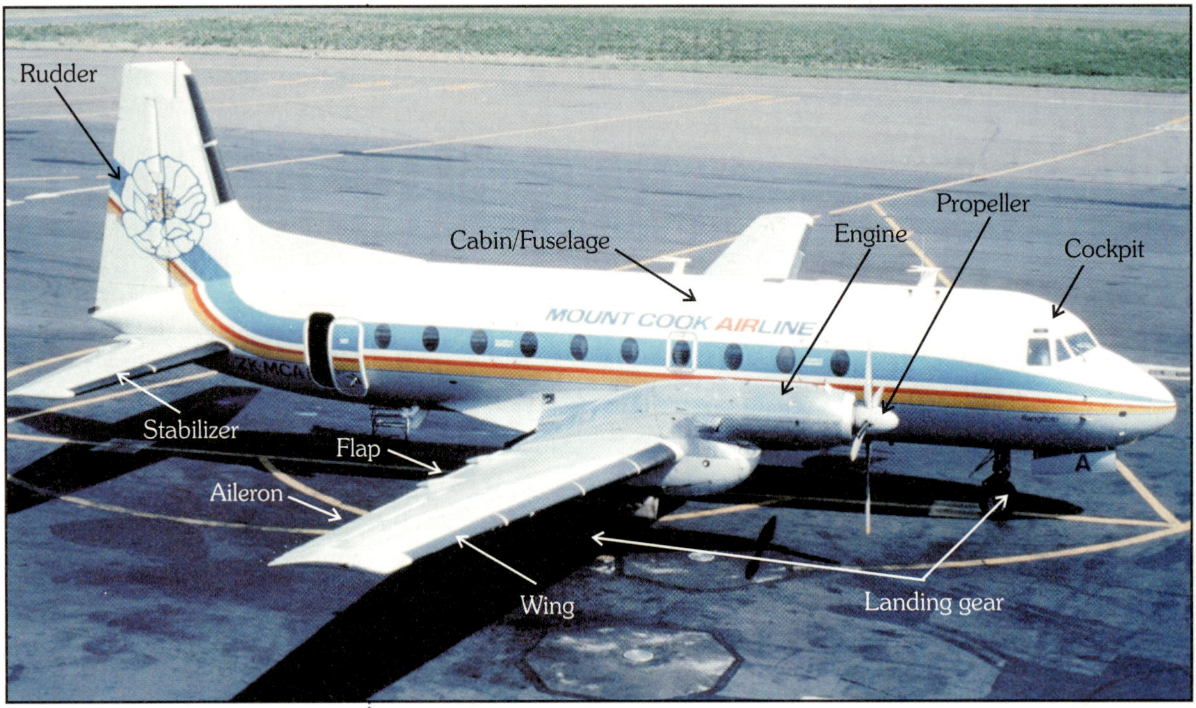

Here are the basic parts of an airplane.

gear helps the pilot land the plane safely and smoothly.

The body of the plane is called the fuselage. Seats for passengers are inside the fuselage of airliners in the passenger cabin. Airliners have small kitchens and rest rooms. The newest 747 has six kitchens and twelve rest rooms. Meals are provided on long flights. On many airliners, passengers can watch movies or listen to music.

Pilots fly the airplane from their cabin.

Sometimes this cabin is called the flight deck or the cockpit. In the pilots' cabin, dials and instruments show how high the airplane is flying. They show how the engines are running and the speed and direction of the plane. Radar and other instruments warn pilots of mountains, bad weather, and other airplanes ahead.

Pilots fly the airplane from their own cabin. This pilot is checking all the controls before take off.

Pilots need to know what each dial, knob, and switch does in a cockpit.

Most modern airliners have a crew of two pilots. Large airliners on long flights bring along an extra pilot. The pilots can take turns flying and resting. Taking off and landing are the two most important jobs for an airplane pilot. Computers help pilots fly most airliners once the plane is in the air.

Airports are places where airplanes land and take off. We need many airports because of the many people who fly each day. Most large cities throughout the world have at least one airport.

There are special buildings called terminal buildings at an airport. A terminal building is a place where passengers sit and wait for their plane. Some terminal buildings have stores and places to eat.

Tickets can be bought at ticket offices in the terminal building. Many people buy their tickets from travel

Inside the terminal building, people wait in line to buy tickets, check their bags, and to make sure their flight is on time (below). Many people work in airports. This ticket agent (inset) is helping a passenger with his ticket.

Screens like these above help people find out when their flight is taking off. People can also find out if an airplane has landed. All bags go through a screening device (inset). You can see what is inside a suitcase on the computer screen.

agents or on the Internet. Passenger tickets and bags are checked in at the ticket desks.

Passengers must walk through a metal detector before going on a plane. This is to make sure that no one is carrying a weapon or anything that could be dangerous onto the plane. Information about different flights is posted on TV screens in the building.

Passenger lists and airplane schedules are

stored in computers. This helps the people in the ticket offices know where everyone is going. Computers list the plane a passenger is taking and when he or she will arrive at the next airport. Computers keep track of the thousands of people who travel each day.

Another large building at an airport is the hangar. A hangar is really an airplane garage. Airplanes that need to be fixed are brought into the hangar.

Hangars are airplane garages. This hangar is big enough to fit two airplanes.

Chapter 5

Many, Many Jobs

There are only a few companies that build big airplanes. But there are many factories that build parts for the airplane companies. Some companies build the instruments used to fly the plane. Others build the landing gear, the wings, the tail, and the fuselage. Some make bolts and other supplies needed to put the plane together. Several companies make the seats and other equipment needed for the passengers. Building airplanes makes jobs for many workers.

Many people at the airport get airplanes ready to fly. Before an airplane can take off, the

Control towers (left) are a very important part of airports and flying.

Many people help build airplanes (inset). Then mechanics help take care of the planes. This mechanic is checking over an airplane engine.

pilot makes a flight plan. This plan shows what route the plane will be flying and how much fuel will be needed for the flight. Mechanics must check the plane over to make sure everything is working correctly. Some workers refuel the plane. Others load the cargo and passengers' bags. Food for the flight must be loaded aboard the plane, and rest rooms must be cleaned.

Workers inside the airport help travelers. Passengers turn in their tickets at the check-in desk at the airport. Tags are put on the bags. The tags have the name of the city where the bags will be sent. All the bags must be checked before they are loaded on the airliner.

The ground crew are workers who guide the airplane into and out of its parking space with lights and hand signals.

Many people work together to make sure passengers' bags are put on the right airplane.

While pilots fly the plane, some men and women look after the passengers. They are called flight attendants. They are trained to tell the passengers what to do in an emergency. They serve meals and snacks. They work hard to keep the passengers comfortable.

At large airports, several planes take off every minute while others land. Airports have a special building called a control tower. Here people called air traffic controllers keep track of airplanes in the air and on the ground. They have radar screens that follow the airplanes. The controllers tell pilots where other airplanes are flying. They tell the pilots which runway to use, and they warn them if bad weather is ahead. Their job is very important. They help keep crowded skies safe.

Airliners need long runways to take off and land. These runways must be kept clean. Any

This 737 plane is parked at a gate and is being prepared for the next flight.

trash on the runway could be very dangerous. In places where it snows in winter, runways must be plowed. All snow and ice must be cleared away before an airliner can take off or land.

Airports have firefighters and fire trucks. They are always ready in case of an emergency in the airport or on the runway.

Thousands of people work hard to keep airplanes flying smoothly and safely.

Many people are needed to keep the skies safe. These people above are working in a control tower. They look at radar screens like this one (inset).

Chapter 6

Newer, Bigger, Better, Faster

Aircraft companies are always trying to make better planes. They look for ways to make them faster, safer, and quieter. It takes years of planning before a new type of plane can be built.

First, engineers are needed to draw up plans for a plane. They build models of the plane. The models are tested in a wind tunnel to see how they will work at different speeds and different pressures. Then only a few planes are built for testing. Today some companies use computers for testing instead of wind tunnels.

Different types of airplanes are tested before they can be used to fly passengers. This is a photo of a cockpit of a 737 (left).

Once a new plane is tested, many can be built. Here, a man is building parts for an airplane.

These mechanics are working on a 727.

Test pilots are the first to fly a new plane. They want to make sure that everything in the plane will work correctly. Test pilots have to fly the plane many times to make sure it is safe. The plane must pass several tests before it is ready for passengers. After the airplane passes all the tests, the plans go to the factory. Now the factory can build many airplanes of this type.

The Boeing 777 is one of the newest and biggest passenger airplanes. Help came from many different places for the plans for this airliner. Engineers working at computers all over the world drew up the plans. This was the first large plane that was built this way. Plans for future planes might be made in the same way.

More and more people are becoming interested in home-built airplanes. Most of these are bought in kits and are put together by the owner. They are used mostly for fun. These planes are lightweight and can carry very few people. They are called experimental aircraft. The Experimental Aircraft Association (EAA) holds a huge convention each year in Oshkosh, Wisconsin. Thousands of pilots and their experimental airplanes come to the convention to learn more about aviation. The EAA runs a Young Eagles program. This program takes

Many people put their own airplanes together. Some of the planes are experimental aircraft, like these. They can be different shapes and sizes.

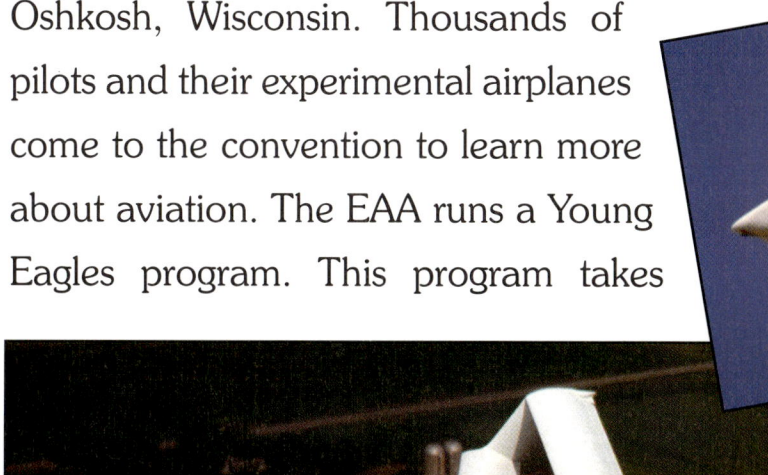

Some companies might have their own small airplanes, like these.

young people flying to show them what it is like to be a pilot.

The Federal Aviation Administration (FAA) must approve all experimental aircraft. There are more experimental airplanes than any other kind of airplane in the world.

Many businesses have their own small airplanes. These planes are used to fly workers to jobs out of town. They are also used to fly people to special meetings in nearby cities. Many companies save time and money by flying their own planes.

Engineers are working on an airliner that does not need a long runway. They want to make a plane that can move nearly straight up and down like a helicopter. This would make it possible for airplanes to go to smaller airports with shorter runways. The armed forces already have some types of these planes.

The next big improvement in airplanes will be spaceplanes. Spaceplanes are often called reusable launch vehicles (RLVs). These planes will have rocket engines. They will fly right through the atmosphere into space. They will fly at over 10,000 miles per hour. That is fifteen times the speed of sound. They will be able to fly almost anywhere in the world in two to three hours. Spaceplanes will probably need much longer runways than our planes do today. Special airports might be needed for spaceplanes.

Many people are coming up with ideas for planes of the future, like this one. It could carry 800 people more than 7,000 miles.

Timeline

1500—Leonardo da Vinci makes drawings of flying machines with wings.

1783—A French scientist, Jean-François Pilâtre de Rozier, becomes the first person to go up in a hot-air balloon.

1903—Orville and Wilbur Wright fly the first engine-powered airplane.

1909—Louis Blériot becomes the first person to fly across the English Channel.

1927—Charles Lindbergh makes the first solo nonstop flight across the Atlantic Ocean.

1932—Amelia Earhart is the first woman to pilot an airplane across the Atlantic Ocean.

1939—The first successful flight of an airplane with a jet engine takes place in Germany.

1952—The world's first large passenger jetliner service begins.

Timeline

1958—The first jet airliner service between the United States and Europe begins.

1968—Russians fly the first supersonic transport jet plane.

1995—The world's largest twin-engine jet, the Boeing 777 airliner, begins passenger service.

Words to Know

aviation—The science of flying airplanes.

cargo—The load of goods carried on a ship or an airplane.

cockpit—The area in the front part of an airplane where the pilots sit and fly the plane.

Federal Aviation Administration (FAA)—The Federal Aviation Administration controls air traffic and sets rules and regulations for airplanes and airports.

fuselage—The body of an airplane.

metal detector—An instrument that shows if a person is carrying a metal object.

pioneer—A person who goes before usually preparing the way for others to follow.

supersonic—Something that travels faster than the speed of sound, which is about 760 mph at sea level.

taxiing—Moving along on the ground on its own power.

terminal building—The building where an airplane trip begins and ends.

Learn More About Airplanes

Books

Graham, Ian. *Aircraft*. New York: Raintree Steck-Vaughn, 1999.

Maynard, Christopher. *Airplanes*. New York: Dorling Kindersley, 1995.

Robinson, Fay. *Pilots Fly Planes*. Chanhassen, Minn.: The Child's World, 1996.

Stille, Darlene. *Airplanes*. New York: Children's Press, 1997.

Internet Addresses

The Federal Aviation Administration: Aviation Education, Kids Corner

<http://www.faa.gov/education/resource/kidcornr.htm>

Click on links for fun, games, and more information about aviation.

How Airplanes Work

<http://www.howstuffworks.com/airplane.htm>

Learn how airplanes fly from this How Stuff Works Web site.

Index

A
Atlantic Ocean, 5, 6, 7, 8
airports, 28–29

B
Blériot, Louis, 22
Boeing 747, 11, 13, 26
Boeing 777, 40
bombers, 22

C
cargo planes, 13
Concorde, 12–13
control tower, 36, 37
crop dusters, 16

D
D'Arlandes, François-Laurent, 20
Da Vinci, Leonardo, 19

E
Earhart, Amelia, 5, 8-9, 44
Electra, 9
English Channel, 22
Experimental Aircraft Association (EAA), 41

F
Federal Aviation Administration (FAA), 42
Flyer, 20–21, 25

H
hangar, 31
hot-air balloon, 19–20

K
Kitty Hawk, North Carolina, 21

L
Lindbergh, Charles A., 5–7

M
Montgolfier brothers, 19

N
New York City, 5, 6
Noonan, Fred, 8

O
Oshkosh, Wisconsin, 41

P
Pacific Ocean, 9

Paris, France, 5, 6, 8
parts of an airplane, 25–27
Pilâtre de Rozier, Jean-François, 20

R
radar, 27
runways, 17, 36, 37, 43

S
seaplane, 16–17
sonic boom, 12
spaceplanes, 43
Spirit of St. Louis, 5

T
terminal buildings, 29

W
World War I, 14, 22
World War II, 14
Wright, Orville, 20–21, 25
Wright, Wilbur, 20–21, 25

Y
Young Eagles, 41–42